# The Sea Maidens of Japan

*For Austin, Lannie, Clara, and Max.*
*Special thanks to the Japan America Society of Colorado*
                                                    *—L. B.*

*For my parents, Betty Jane and Bob, with all my love.*
                                                    *—E. M. B.*

Text copyright © 1996 by Lili Bell
Illustrations copyright © 1996 by Hambleton-Hill Publishing, Inc.

Published by Ideals Children's Books
An imprint of Hambleton-Hill Publishing, Inc.
Nashville, Tennessee 37218

Printed and bound in the United States of America

**Library of Congress Cataloging-in-Publication Data**
Bell, Lili, 1956–
    The sea maidens of Japan / by Lili Bell ; illustrated by Erin
McGonigle Brammer.
        p.   cm.
    Summary: A young Japanese girl struggles to meet the expectations
of her mother and the unique culture of the sea divers who capture
food for their village.
    ISBN 1-57102-095-0 (hardcover)
    [I. Japan—Fiction. 2. Fishers—Fiction. 3. Women—Employment—
Fiction.] I. Brammer, Erin McGonigle, ill. II. Title.
PZ7.B38925Se      1996
[E]—dc20                                              96-16132
                                                         CIP
                                                          AC

The illustrations in this book were rendered in oil wash and colored pencil
    using live models.
The text type was set in Cochin.
The display type was set in Ingenius.
Color separations were made by Color 4, Inc.
Printed and bound by Bertelsmann Corporation.

First Edition

10 9 8 7 6 5 4 3 2 1

# The Sea Maidens of Japan

By Lili Bell

Illustrated by
Erin McGonigle Brammer

Ideals Children's Books
Nashville, Tennessee
an imprint of Hambleton-Hill Publishing, Inc.

We are called the *ama*, the sea maidens of Japan. My mother's mother and even her great-grandmother's mother were fisherwomen who dove to the ocean floor to harvest seafood for the great emperors of Japan.

When I'm older, I'll learn to hold my breath under water for over a minute and gather abalone and seaweed for my family and our village. Okaasan, that is what I call my mama, teaches me to dive and fish along the shallow reefs.

"Kiyomi, when you're older and follow our tradition," she tells me, "you will not have the rope attached to your waist. You must find your own way without me."

Hearing this, my stomach flutters. I must not disgrace Okaasan and fail because I am afraid of the deep waters. I long to be a brave ama diver, but I don't want to be swallowed up by the dark, deep waters.

My two older sisters chose the modern way of life and work in the city at the fish canneries. They will not become ama, like Okaasan and me.

While my mother dives, I wait alone for long hours on the shore of a special cove. On this coral beach, every grain of sand is shaped like a star. Sitting in a shallow pool, I pretend to host tea ceremonies for mermaids. I chase schools of fish away from my treasure chest. At the end of the day, I wait for Okaasan and count the stars on the beach and in the sky.

In the middle of the night, Okaasan wakes me. "Come, Kiyomi, the sea turtles will lay their eggs on the beach tonight," she whispers. It is hard for me to open my eyes. Gently shaking my shoulder, she says, "Wake up, little one, the sea turtles come only once a year."

The moon is bright and the sky sparkles with stars. Gusts of wind sting my cheeks, leaving a strong, salty taste in my mouth. As each wave pounds at the shore, the ocean roars and foams like a terrible dragon. We wait a long time. I poke a stick at a pile of strong-smelling sea kelp circled with flies. I feel like a tiny fly next to the great power of the ocean.

Perhaps the ocean is too rough for the turtles to come. As we head home, rain clouds veil the starlight. The sky is so dark that I trip over pieces of driftwood. Okaasan waits for me and places her warm hand in mine.

Just then, with each incoming wave, the sea turtles begin to appear. They are graceful and smooth in the water. On land they struggle, slow and awkward, onto the beach to select a nesting spot. I cup my hand over my mouth to hush my giggling as they dig a hole with their hind flippers and spray sand in each other's faces.

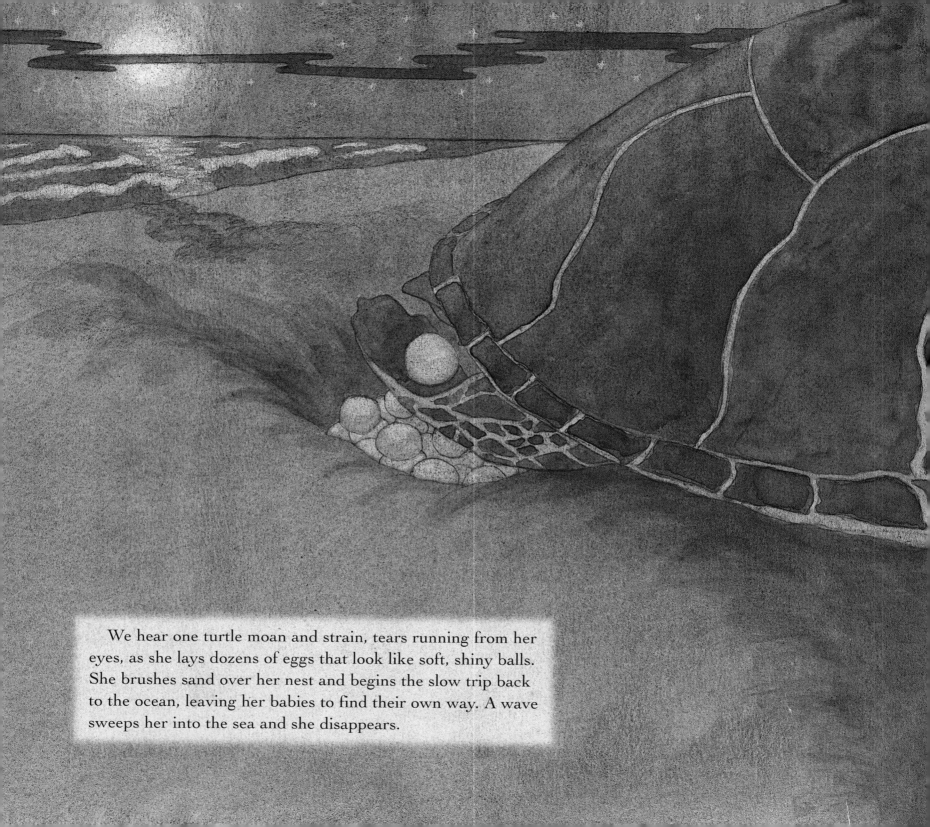

We hear one turtle moan and strain, tears running from her eyes, as she lays dozens of eggs that look like soft, shiny balls. She brushes sand over her nest and begins the slow trip back to the ocean, leaving her babies to find their own way. A wave sweeps her into the sea and she disappears.

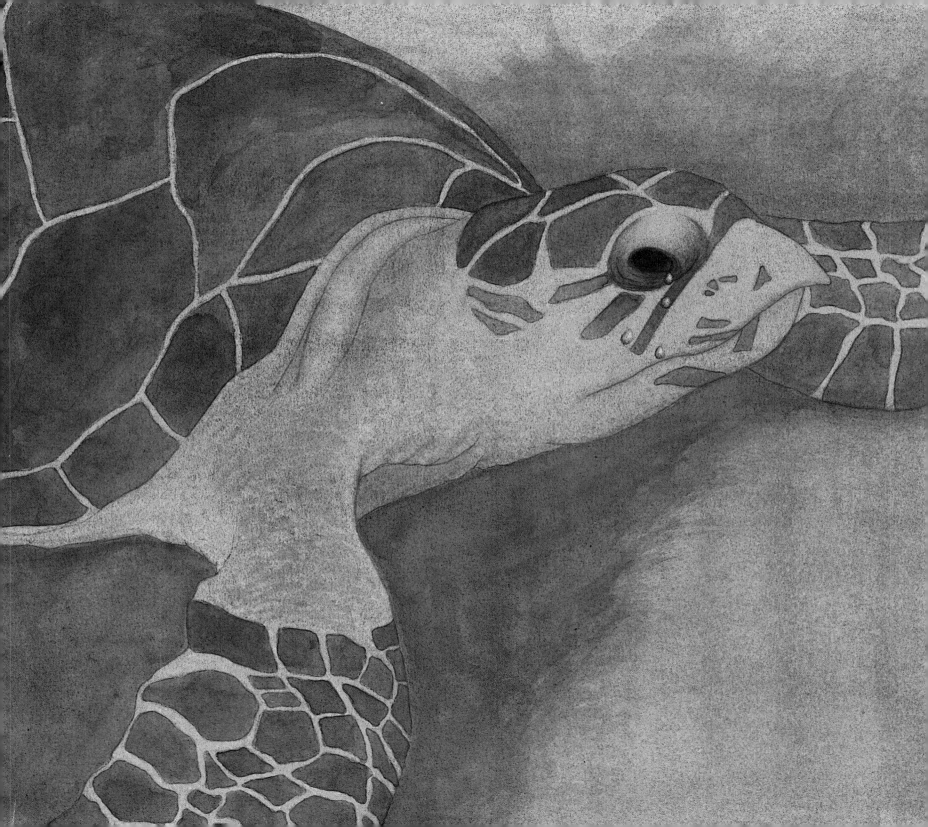

Every day I visit the beach to check the nests. The sun soaks the sand with warmth for the eggs to grow. Some eggs are scooped up in the fishermen's buckets. Others are eaten by hungry birds and crabs, but I try to chase them away.

After two full moons pass, I see a nest hatch on the star cove. Out of the sand pops a tiny flipper, a head, and then an entire body. Ten, twelve, fifteen little turtles emerge from the depths of the star sand and scurry toward the ocean.

One confused baby turtle runs in the wrong direction—away from the water! He scrambles toward the soft orange light that glows from the paper lanterns in the village. I run after the little turtle and pick him up. On his shell is the shape of a grain of star sand. He flails his neck and flippers. Gently, I guide the frightened turtle to the shoreline. A huge wave swallows him and carries him out to the deep sea.

I wonder if the star turtle is strong enough to survive. I wonder, too, if I am strong enough to be an ama diver.

Several fishing seasons come and go. The time arrives for me to make a deep water dive with the ama. I try, but I cannot peel my feet off the boat deck to jump into the dark, murky water. Okaasan sighs and looks down, away from me. To my despair, I hear muffled giggles.

At night I toss and turn in bed like a fish caught in a net. I get up, look out the window, and see the faint glow of the city lights. My mind is set. I will run to the city and find my sisters rather than embarrass Okaasan any further.

Okaasan is quiet as she serves our breakfast. Finally she says, "Kiyomi, you will come with me to the ama boats today."

Cupping my soup bowl in both hands, I take a sip but can barely taste or swallow.

"Kiyomi-chan, you must keep trying," she says.

At the dock, the ama prepare for a day of work. We put white cream on my face to protect it from the cold, salty water. Moments later, the boats creep through a thick fog, farther from the village than I've ever been. Almost ready to dive, I look at the black water and begin to shake.

Something moves in the water, but I cannot see what it is. A drum pounds in my chest. I look at Okaasan and she nods at me firmly. Again, I see something move in the water. This time, I see the outline of a turtle. My heart leaps. Could it be the star turtle?

I take a deep breath and blow through pursed lips, sounding like the distant cry of a gull on a wind-swept beach. I hold in another breath, force my feet off the deck, and dive.

Stroking the water furiously, I try to keep up with the sea turtle. As he swoops deeper to the ocean floor, I recognize the star on his shell. Grabbing his shell, we rise together to the surface for air. I turn loose, tread water, and watch the turtle gracefully swim away.

All morning I dive deep, hunt for abalone, and pry them off the rocks with my knife. When I return to the boats, all the ama are pleased.

"Today, Kiyomi, you have become an ama," Okaasan says proudly.

On a small island beach we collect firewood and dry leaves. Women, wrapped in thin, white clothing, huddle around the fire as shellfish sizzle in the embers. I cannot tell if I tremble from the cold or excitement. My skin is swollen and pale. An older ama places a blanket on my shoulders. With chopsticks, we pick the flavorful fish from the shells.

In the surf, I see the star turtle bobbing in the water, watching me. I smile at my friend as a huge wave sweeps him into the deep waters. On this island beach I sit for the first time among the brave ama, the sea maidens of Japan.

# 海女

## Author's Note

The *ama* are Japanese sea divers who hunt for fish, shellfish, and seaweed without the aid of underwater breathing apparatus. Most of the ama are women, particularly in the fishing communities of central Japan. The *kachido,* "walking people," dive in shallow water from the shore and toss their catch into floating wooden tubs. The *funado,* "ship people," are older and more experienced and dive in deeper waters from an anchored boat. The ama hunt mostly for *awabi* (abalone), *sazae* (wreath shell snail), *tengusa* (agar-agar), and *eganori* (a kind of edible seaweed). The ama's method of diving was first recorded by Chinese observers in Japan during the third century.

### Pronunciation Guide

| | |
|---|---|
| abalone | ab-a-lo-nee |
| ama | a-ma |
| awabi | a-wa-bee |
| eganori | e-ga-no-ree |
| funado | fu-na-do |
| kachido | ka-chee-do |
| Kiyomi | Kee-yo-mee |
| Okaasan | O-ka-a-san |
| sazae | sa-za-e |
| tengusa | ten-gu-sa |